The Hut that Grew

Annie Dalton

Illustrated by Laura Clark

A & C Black • London

White Wolves series consultant: Sue Ellis,
Centre for Literacy in Primary Education

This book can be used in the White Wolves Guided Reading
programme by more advanced readers in Year 2

The rights of Annie Dalton and Laura Clark to be identified
as the author and illustrator of this work has been asserted by them
in accordance with the Copyrights, Designs and Patents Act 1988.

ISBN 978-1-4081-2650-9

A CIP catalogue for this book is available from the British Library.

This book is produced using paper that is made from wood
grown in managed, sustainable forests. It is natural, renewable
and recyclable. The logging and manufacturing processes conform
to the environmental regulations of the country of origin.

Printed and bound in China by C&C Offset Printing Co.

Chapter One

There once was a princess who lived in a palace in Ethiopia. Inside the shining golden walls, Princess Zima felt safe and happy. Her parents loved her and gave her everything she wanted.

Then, one day, her father had some
bad news.

"We've lost all our money," he said.
"We must leave the palace at once."

"But where will we live?" gasped the
princess.

"We can move into the gatekeeper's hut,"
said the queen. "It's not so bad. Come on,
we'll show you."

The princess was in shock. The palace, with its marble floors and tinkling fountains, was the only home she had ever known.

The gatekeeper's hut had a straw roof and smelled of chickens.

The princess burst into tears. "There's nowhere to put my stuff. Don't make us live here, Daddy! I'll die!"

The king and queen didn't know how to make things better. They just walked away, leaving her sobbing.

All at once, Princess Zima heard a voice singing a strange little song.

"I know a way to dry your eyes. I know a way to cure your sorrow."

A magician must have heard about our troubles! she thought. Wiping away her tears, she ran out of the hut.

Chapter Two

Princess Zima hurried through the palace
gates and looked up and down the dusty
street. She couldn't see anyone who looked
like a magician. There was just an old
man sitting under a fig tree. Nearby, three
chickens scratched around in the dirt.

"Good morning, Uncle," the princess said politely. "Was that you singing?"

The old man smiled. "It was."

"Can you really help me?" asked the princess.

"I can and I will," said the old man. "But you must promise to do everything I tell you, no matter how strange."

"If you can turn that horrible hut into a home fit for a princess, I'll do anything you say," she promised.

The old man smiled. "Just take these chickens home to live with you."

"That's easy!" said the princess, and off she ran.

The sun was setting as the family moved into the hut. The king and queen were surprised when their daughter appeared with three chickens, but they didn't say a word. They were just pleased to see the princess happy again.

That night, the princess lay down on her sleeping mat and smiled. *When I wake up, this hut will be a home fit for a princess,* she thought. Next morning, Princess Zima found a chicken sitting on her head, and the hut was still a hut.

This was disappointing, but the princess wasn't giving up. *I'll go back to the old man,* she thought. *Maybe he can tell me what went wrong.*

Chapter Three

Princess Zima found the old man sitting under the fig tree. A white goat was tied up nearby.

"I did what you said, but the hut is still a hut. Please tell me how to make the magic work," she begged.

The old man smiled. "There aren't enough animals in the hut," he said. "Take this goat home with you."

The king and queen whispered together when they saw their daughter arrive with a goat, but they did nothing.

"Zima is happy, that's the main thing," the king said to his wife.

14

That night, the princess lay down on her sleeping mat and smiled. *When I wake up, this hut will be a home fit for a princess,* she thought.

Next morning, Princess Zima found the goat eating her favourite red dress, and the hut was still a hut.

I don't understand. Why isn't the magic working? she thought. *Maybe the old man can tell me what went wrong.*

The princess found him under his fig tree, as usual. A donkey was tied up nearby.

"I did what you said, but the hut is still a hut. Please tell me how to make the magic work," she pleaded.

"There are still not enough animals in the hut. You need this donkey," the old man told her.

When Princess Zima led the donkey inside the hut, the queen gave a gasp.

"I didn't say anything about the chickens or the goat, but a donkey is too much," she whispered to her husband.

"Don't be so hasty," the king whispered back. "Things might work out."

That night, Princess Zima lay down on her sleeping mat between the donkey and the goat. She didn't smile. She felt too squashed. Also, the chicken feathers made her sneeze. *When I wake up, this hut will be a home fit for a- a- a- tishoo!* she sneezed.

Next morning, Princess Zima heard a loud *HEE-HAW!* in her ear. There were chicken feathers and goat mess everywhere. The hut was still a hut. The princess didn't know what to do. Was the old man playing tricks on her?

Chapter Four

Princess Zima found the old man sitting under his fig tree. A family of monkeys was playing in the branches.

"I think you're playing tricks on me, Uncle," she said. "I did what you told me, but things are getting worse!"

The old man smiled. "When things get worse, it means the magic is starting to work."

This was such good news, the princess clapped her hands. "Please tell me what to do next," she begged.

"You need even more animals in the hut. Take these monkeys home with you," said the old man.

He whistled. The monkeys climbed down from the tree and followed Princess Zima back to the hut.

When the queen saw them coming, she folded her arms. "I refuse to share my home with monkeys," she told her husband. "This has to stop!"

"Keep quiet just a little longer," begged the king.

That night, the princess couldn't sleep.
The baby monkey kept kicking and pinching,
and his brothers and sisters took Princess
Zima's blanket. But she didn't complain.
Tomorrow, this hut will be a home fit for a princess,
she told herself.

But when the sun rose the next day,
the hut was still a hut.

All at once, Princess Zima was FURIOUS! She marched out of the palace gates. The old man was smiling to himself under the fig tree. A skinny old camel was tied up nearby.

"Stop smiling!" the princess shouted. "I've done everything you told me, and the hut is still a hut. And *don't* tell me to take that old camel home. The place is so full, there's no room for a *mouse*!"

The old man frowned. "You promised to do everything I tell you, but as soon as it gets hard, you change your mind."

That's true, thought the princess. *I never had to do anything hard when I lived in the palace.*

She walked home thoughtfully leading the camel.

Chapter Five

That night was the worst night of the
princess's life. The chickens walked over her.
The goat ate her blanket. The donkey went
HEE-HAW! HEE-HAW! The monkeys kept
kicking her out of bed, and the camel's
breath smelled *horrible*.

When morning came, Princess Zima didn't even look. She could tell from the dreadful smells that the hut was still a hut, and she burst into tears.

She limped through the palace gates to find the old man. She couldn't run because the goat had taken a big bite out of her shoe and it kept falling off.

"I did everything you told me, Uncle, but the hut is still a hut. Please, *please* tell me what I'm doing wrong," she sobbed.

The old man smiled. "You did everything *right*, princess. Now you will get your reward. Go back to the hut and shoo all those animals away."

Princess Zima didn't need telling twice.
She ran home and did what the old man said.
She chased the last chicken out of the door,
then she went back inside ... and gasped.

The magic had worked!

Without the chickens, the goat, the
donkey, the monkeys and the skinny old
camel, the little hut felt ENORMOUS!

Princess Zima laughed out loud because the old man had played a trick on her after all, an extremely *clever* trick.

"I knew things would work out," the king whispered to the queen.

Princess Zima started to dance, because this was Africa, where people dance when they're happy, and her parents joined in.

And though they couldn't see him, the old man was dancing, too.